ALFIE

Alfie Gets in First

For Jamie and Henry

Other titles in the Alfie series:

Alfie's Feet
Alfie Gives a Hand
An Evening at Alfie's
Alfie and the Birthday Surprise
Alfie Wins a Prize
Alfie and the Big Boys
Alfie Weather
Alfie's World
Annie Rose is my Little Sister
Rhymes for Annie Rose
The Big Alfie and Annie Rose Storybook
The Big Alfie Out of Doors Storybook

ALFIE GETS IN FIRST
A RED FOX BOOK 978 1 782 95415 6

First published in Great Britain by The Bodley Head, an imprint of Random House Children's Publishers UK
A Random House Group Company

The Bodley Head edition published 1981
Red Fox edition first published 1991
This Red Fox edition published 2014

1 3 5 7 9 10 8 6 4 2

Copyright © Shirley Hughes, 1981

Red Fox Books are published by Random House Children's Publishers UK,
61–63 Uxbridge Road, London W5 5SA

www.randomhousechildrens.co.uk
www.randomhouse.co.uk

Addresses for companies within The Random House Group Limited can be found at: www.randomhouse.co.uk/offices.htm

THE RANDOM HOUSE GROUP Limited Reg. No. 954009

A CIP catalogue record for this book is available from the British Library.

Printed in China

ALFIE

Alfie Gets in First

Shirley Hughes

Red Fox

One day Alfie and Mum and Annie Rose were coming home from the shops. Alfie ran on ahead because he wanted to get home first. He ran all the way from the corner to the front gate and up the steps to the front door.

Then he sat down on the top step and waited for the others. Along came Mum, pushing Annie Rose and the shopping.

"I raced you!" called Alfie. "I'm back first, so there!"

Annie Rose didn't care. She was tired. She sat back in her push-chair and sucked her thumb.

Mum put the brake on the push-chair and
left Annie Rose at the bottom of the steps
while she lifted the basket of shopping up to
the top. Then she found the key and opened
the front door. Alfie dashed in ahead of her.

"I've won, I've won!" he shouted.

Mum put the shopping down in the hall and went
back down the steps to lift Annie Rose out of her
push-chair. But what do you think Alfie did then?

He gave the door a great big slam – BANG!
– just like that.

Then Mum was outside the door, holding
Annie Rose, and Alfie was inside with the
shopping. Mum's key was inside too.

"Open the door, Alfie," said Mum.

But Alfie didn't know how to open the door from the inside. The catch was too high up. Mum looked into the letter-box.

"Try to reach the catch and turn it," she said. Alfie tried but he couldn't quite reach it.

"Can you put the key through the letter-box?" said Mum. But Alfie couldn't reach the letter-box either.

Annie Rose was hungry as well as tired. She began to cry. Then Alfie began to cry too. He didn't like being all by himself on the wrong side of the door. Just then Mrs MacNally came hurrying across the street to see what all the noise was about.

She and Mum took it in turns to say
encouraging things into the letter-box.
But Alfie still couldn't open the door.

"Go and fetch your little chair from the sitting-room and then you'll be able to reach the catch," said Mum. But Alfie didn't try to fetch his little chair. He just went on crying, louder and louder, and Annie Rose cried louder and louder too.

"There's my Maureen," said Mrs MacNally. "I'm sure she'll be able to help."

Mrs MacNally's Maureen was a big girl. Right
away she came and joined Mum and Annie Rose and
Mrs MacNally on the top step.

"Mmm, might have to break a window," she
said. "But I'll try to climb up the drain-pipe
first, if you like."

But Mrs MacNally didn't like that idea at all.

"Oh no, Maureen, you might hurt yourself," she said.

Just then Alfie's very good friend the milkman came
up the street in his milk-float.

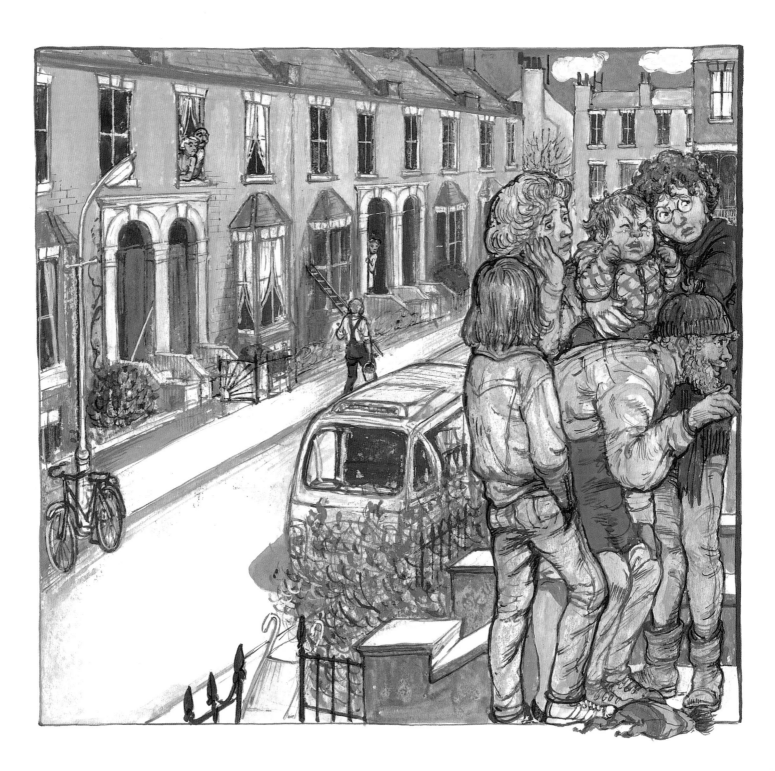

When he saw Mum and Annie Rose and Mrs MacNally
and Mrs MacNally's Maureen all standing on the top
step he stopped his float and said:

"What's the trouble?"

So they told him.

"Don't worry, mate," the milkman shouted. "We'll
soon have you out of there."

"Mmm, looks as though this lock's going to be difficult to break," said the milkman. But then Mrs MacNally's Maureen had a very good idea. She ran to ask the window-cleaner, who was working up the street, if he would bring his ladder and climb up to the bathroom window. And, of course, when the window-cleaner heard about Alfie he came hurrying along with his ladder as quickly as he could.

Then Mum and Annie Rose and Mrs MacNally and
Mrs MacNally's Maureen and the milkman all stood on
the top step and watched while the window-cleaner put
his ladder up against the house. He started to climb
up to the bathroom window. But when he was half-way
up the ladder, what do you think happened?

The front door suddenly opened and there
was Alfie! He had managed to reach the catch
and turn it – like that – after all.

He was *very* pleased with himself.
He opened the front door
as wide as it would go and
stood back grandly to let
everybody in.

Then the window-cleaner came down from his
ladder, and he and the milkman and Mrs MacNally's
Maureen and Mrs MacNally and Annie Rose and Mum
and Alfie all went into the kitchen and had tea together.